Inky-pinky
blot

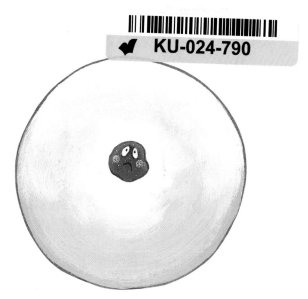

by Judith Nicholls
illustrated by Tim Warnes

Ladybird

George was sad.

He couldn't jump,
he couldn't jiggle.
He couldn't run,
he couldn't wriggle.

All he could do was dream...
drifting by the weeds
in the dark, dark, pond.

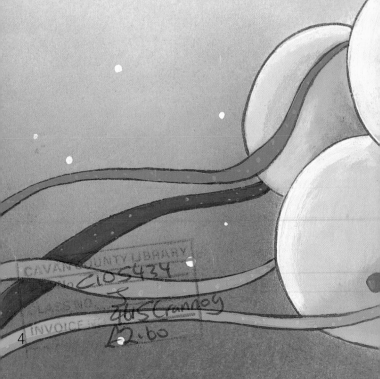

4

Here's a story to share!

Sharing a story with your child is great fun and it's an ideal way to start your child reading.

The left-hand pages are 'your' story pages. The right-hand pages are specially written for your child with simple vocabulary and helpful repetition.

• Cuddle up close and look through the book together. What's happening in the pictures?

• Read the whole story to your child, both your story pages and your child's. Tell your child what it says on his* story pages and point to the words as you say them.

• Now it's time to read the story again and see if your child would like to join in and read his story pages along with you. Don't worry about perfect reading – what matters at this stage is having fun.

• It's best to stop when your child wants to. You can pick up the book at any time and enjoy sharing the story all over again.

Here the child is referred to as 'he'. All Ladybird books are equally suitable for both boys and girls.

Edited by Lorraine Horsley and Caroline Rashleigh
Designed by Alison Guthrie, Lara Stapleton and Graeme Hole
A catalogue record for this book is available from the British Library
Published by Ladybird Books Ltd
27 Wrights Lane London W8 5TZ
A Penguin Company
2 4 6 8 10 9 7 5 3 1
TEXT © JUDITH NICHOLLS MMI
ILLUSTRATIONS © TIM WARNES MMI
This story was previously published by Ladybird as Who Am I? MCMXCVI
LADYBIRD and the device of a Ladybird are trademarks of Ladybird Books Ltd

George was sad.

"Who am I?"
he asked the water-boatman.
The water-boatman was
far too busy to stop.
He stared crossly.

"Who are you?
You're a dot,
you're a spot,
you're a jelly-belly tot.
You're an inky-pinky blot
in the dark, dark pond!"

"Who am I?" said George.

The water-boatman kicked his
legs proudly, and darted away
through the weedy water.

George was sad.

He couldn't dart,
he couldn't hop.
He couldn't start,
he couldn't stop.

All he could do was dream...
drifting by the weeds
in the dark, dark pond.

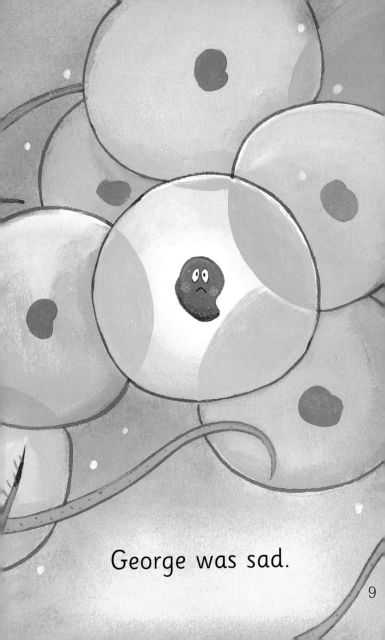

George was sad.

"Who am I?" he asked the stickleback.
The stickleback wriggled closer,
then she giggled.

"Who are you?
You're a dot,
you're a spot,
you're a jelly-belly tot.
You're an inky-pinky blot
in the dark, dark pond!"

"Who am I?" said George.

The stickleback flicked her tail proudly,
and danced away through the
weedy water.

George waited sadly.

He couldn't dance,
he couldn't kick.
He couldn't glide,
he couldn't flick.

But each day he grew just
a little bigger...

and bigger...

and bigger...

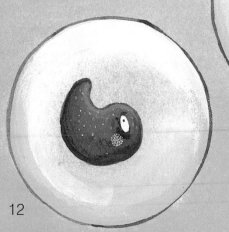

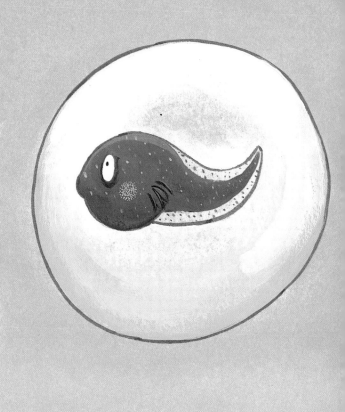

He got bigger and bigger
and bigger.

One day the stickleback wriggled
past again.

"Fiddle-my-fins,
fiddle-my-fins –
you're getting fat!
And fiddle-my-
fiddledy-diddledy-fins –
just what do you think
is THAT?"

"What is that?"

George looked behind
to find a...

TAIL!

He waved it,
he wiggled it.
He flicked it,
he jiggled it.

"Now who am I?" he asked in excitement.

"Pooh! I've already told you that,"
said the stickleback, rudely.

"You're a dot,
you're a spot,
you're a jelly-belly tot.
You're an inky-pinky blot
in the dark, dark pond!"

"Who am I?" said George.

"I'm not!" cried George.
"I'm not, I'm not, I'm NOT!"

And this time,
to his surprise,
he darted forward.

The stickleback
wriggled off in alarm.

Each day George grew bigger...

and bigger...

and bigger...

He got bigger and bigger
and bigger.

One day the water-boatman
darted by again.
When he saw George this time
he stopped and stared.
He looked puzzled.

"What is this?
You're not a dot
or a spot!
You're not a jelly-belly tot
any longer."

"What is this?"

George looked behind to find...

LEGS!

He looked, he kicked,
he licked his lips.

The water-boatman darted off in alarm,
and George kicked again.

He landed rather breathlessly
on a slithery, sunny rock by the edge
of the dark, dark pond.
He stared around. Then he smiled
and blinked happily.

"I can do it!"

"I can do it!" said George.

"I can dance, I can kick,
I can glide, I can flick!

I can jump, I can jiggle,
I can race, I can wriggle!

I can swim, I can hop,
I can jelly-belly flop!"

"I can dance. I can kick,"
said George.

"I can leap to a leaf,
I can dive to a log!

I can slide, I can hide,
I am ME! I am...

FROG!"

"I am me!" said George.

Turn off the TV, close the door, too.
Here's a story to share for just me and you...

Inky-pinky blot

Who is the inky-pinky blot in the dark, dark
pond? He asks everyone who goes by, but
no one ever seems to know…

Caterpillars can't fly!

A baby caterpillar dreams of flying high
in the sky but all her friends just laugh.
What is she to do?

By the light of the Moon

Charlie the zoo keeper has gone home and
the zoo is quiet. Now it's time for the animals to
dance by the light of the moon…

Molly Maran and the Fox

It's cold outside and Molly the kind-hearted
hen says all the animals can stay in her warm
barn. But how will she keep out the wily fox?